MALDIVES

&

MISTLETOE

A CHICAGO WAR CHRISTMAS NOVELLA

BETHANY-KRIS

Published by Bethany-Kris

www.bethanykris.com

ISBN 13: 978-1-988197-76-0

Cover Art © Sasha Elle

Editor: Elizabeth Peters

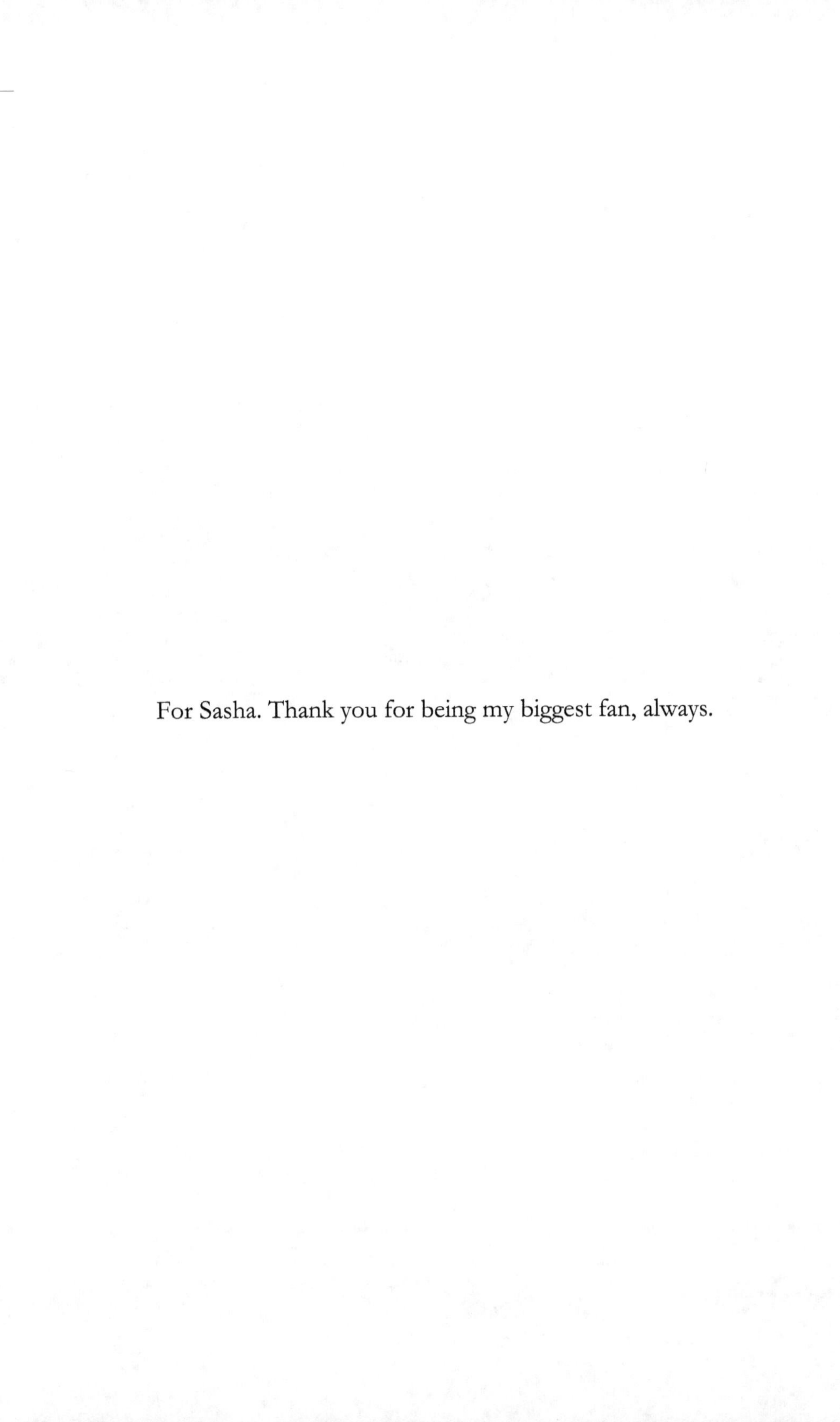

For Sasha. Thank you for being my biggest fan, always.

CONTENTS

ONE

Lily and Damian

LILY

Holidays shouldn't be stressful. Of that, Lily Rossi was *most* sure. They shouldn't draw anxiety into a person's heart beyond deciding which gift to buy for someone. A person should only have to worry about showing up on time to parties, eating good food, and relaxing.

Holidays should not involve packing luggage for two kids—two *very* rowdy toddler boys, as a matter of fact—one tired mother, and a father who looked like he was at the end of his rope.

"*Why* do you need all that?" Damian asked from the bedroom doorway.

Lily huffed, and blew a stray wave of her blonde hair out of her eye as she leaned over the suitcase, and tried her damnedest to squish the contents down just enough to finally—maybe, by the grace of God—get the top zipped. "Instead of opening your mouth to ask stupid questions," she growled at her husband, "why don't you get over here and help me close this?"

"Lily," Damian returned calmly, "it's going to be overweight."

"So, we'll pay the extra. What do you want me to do? You know how Joe and Cory are—they need all the clothes or they'll have *no fucking clothes.*"

Because boys were messy.

And *loud.*

Plus, the boys needed their favorite toys. Things to keep them occupied on the plane, and off it. Kids also just had to travel with a lot of shit because they were kids and that's how life treated parents. Like one big *joke.*

Haha, so funny.

Not to mention, if Lily didn't remember to pack things for her husband, Damian would have nothing to wear because he didn't give a shit. He would rather concern himself over what kind of food he was going to get on the plane rather than what he was going to wear when they got to the Maldives.

So yes, Lily had to pack a whole lot of crap for only a few people.

"*Ma! Cory takes my toy! Ma!*"

Lily grunted, and shook her head as she ignored the shout of her three-year-old coming from down the hall. Joe hated people in his space. Already, at his age, he just wanted to be left alone to do his own thing, and on his own time. If he wanted to join people or a party, then he would do that. But more often than not, Lily would find her son in a quiet space playing on his own.

It was just what he liked.

Joe reminded Lily a lot of his father in that way.

Cory, on the other hand?

Oh, that child was the complete opposite. He *needed* attention.

Thrived on it, really. The two-year-old wanted to be the center of every person's universe, and fuck you if you thought you were going to do as much as take a piss without him talking to you throughout the whole endeavor.

Lily loved her kids.

Loved them with her whole heart, to the ends of the earth and back … until she took her very last breath, and even then … she would keep on loving them.

But this motherhood thing?

This was no fucking joke.

It was not for the weak of heart, or those with queasy stomachs. Motherhood would chew up the weak, and spit them out the other side with messy hair, smudged makeup, and dried *something* on their shoulder before they even realized what happened.

Kids were like sharks in the water. They could smell your blood for the weakness it was. And when they smelled that … you were done for. There was no saving you from them.

"*Ma*!"

Damian sighed, and shoved his hands in his pockets as he rocked back on his heels just enough to stare down the hallway outside the bedroom. "Joe, you handle your brother. You know the rules. Get along, or don't. But *you* handle it."

"But—"

"*Joe*."

"He takes my toys!"

"Handle your brother."

Lily swore not five seconds later, she heard a *thwack* that echoed in the hallway. Following that was the disbelieving screech of pain from a two-year-old before another *thwack* followed.

"Ow, Cory. No hit me!"

"No hits!" Cory shouted.

Thwack. Thwack. Thwack.

"No hits!"

The battle between toddlers continued raging on down the hall, but neither Lily or Damian moved to stop it. Damian sighed again, and gave his wife a look that spoke volumes without actually having to say anything at all.

That was the thing about their kids. If they stepped in to stop every petty argument, then the boys would always depend on their parents to handle whatever issues came up between them. They were close in age—only a year separated them—so they had to learn to make room for each other in their lives, share their spaces, and be *brothers*.

Right now, it was toys and they were two and three. But what about when they were sixteen and seventeen, and it was something bigger than toys?

They had to figure out petty nonsense alone.

"Whose idea was this again to leave Chicago for Christmas, take all the kids to the Maldives, and *hope* it would be okay?" Lily asked.

Damian chuckled dryly. "I think you mean *pray* it would be okay, sweetheart."

Another screech echoed. Another *thwack* followed. Lily sent up a silent thanks for the fact she had a few years to go before she would have to worry about any more kids given that damn IUD she had put in after Cory was born.

She was not having more kids until the two she had learned to get along. Although, according to everyone else, that was never going to happen. Regardless of what Damian and Lily tried to do to make their sons work out their issues and get along, this was just what siblings did.

They would fight their way into adulthood, and annoy the hell out of their parents the whole time. Might as well just sit back, and enjoy the ride. There wasn't anything they could do about it, and they would only drive themselves crazy trying.

"Seriously," Lily said as she *finally* got the overstuffed luggage zipped and stood straight with another huff, "whose brilliant idea was it to take all these kids, shove them on a plane, and fly for hours with the hope that it would be fantastic?"

Damian shrugged. "Theo and Eve. Well, they suggested we take the kids, too, and the wives. Adriano made the deal for this time of the year, and all."

Of course, Theo and Eve had thought putting these kids on a plane instead of a private jet would be a good idea.

The only childless ones in the bunch.

"Remind me to give them the *worst* Christmas present," Lily muttered. "But an especially bad one for my dumbass brother."

Damian smirked as he turned to head into the hallway and handle the kids. "Hell, Lily, I will help you pick it out."

She had no doubt.

TWO

Alessa and Adriano

ALESSA

"I'm sorry, sir, but there's something wrong with this barcode," the woman behind the desk said, trying once again to unsuccessfully scan the ticket Adriano had printed off. "It looks like it may have been smudged a bit. If you have the email—"

Alessa could feel Adriano's stress picking up from two feet away. It practically vibrated off her husband. All the while, she attempted to keep their two young daughters occupied and happy enough to stay quiet. But they were toddlers, so that was a failed fucking effort, too. Life had a way of playing jokes on people at the worst times.

"I don't have the email," Adriano muttered.

The woman behind the check-ins desk lifted a brow. "Why not?"

That was a perfectly reasonable question with a perfectly horrible answer. Because of life. And jokes. This time, the goddamn joke was on them.

"My phone made its way into the toilet this morning," Adriano said, sighing as he scrubbed a hand down his face. "Someone thought it needed cleaning. I had already printed off the ticket, and wasn't bringing my laptop along for this trip, so no, I don't have the damn email."

The woman's gaze drifted to where Alessa stood just a couple of feet back with one toddler balanced on her waist, and another tugging on her hand because Corrine had found something shiny or pretty she liked and wanted to go get it *right now*. Which she kept repeating loudly. That was the thing about toddlers. They didn't give a shit about anything. They had no concept of good or bad behavior. They only had needs and wants, and they didn't understand the difference between the two things at all.

Sympathy stared back from the woman as Alessa shrugged as if to silently say, *What can you do*?

Life rarely went as planned.

Alessa had learned to plan for these things over time, but she'd dropped the ball today. Usually, she'd have the backups for everything paperwork wise just in case. But the baby had ended up having a puking fit the night before, and she'd panicked thinking they wouldn't be able to fly the next day. All of her attention went to making sure the baby didn't have any kind of bug, and finishing up last minute packing.

So, here they were.

Kind of screwed.

"Okay, give me a few minutes," the woman said, taking the printed ticket from Adriano's hand. "Leave your IDs with me, and the card used to buy the ticket. I will put all these reference numbers in, double check everything, and we'll get you on the flight. It's just going to take a bit more time than usual."

Adriano let out a noise that sounded a hell of a lot like relief, but Alessa couldn't be sure. That was the thing—when everything seemed to be going well, something was quick to jump in and laugh in their faces before it all went to shit.

Her husband turned to give her a smile as the woman got to work. Alessa winked, trying to make Adriano smile a bit. It worked, like it usually did. He reached out to stroke a hand over the downy soft hair of their youngest's head as he came close enough to drop a kiss on the top of Alessa's head.

"What a morning, huh?"

"It'll get sorted. We'll make the flight."

Everyone else had already checked in, dropped off their bags, and went through security. They had probably gotten food, made sure all the kids were happy and settled, and were currently waiting at the gate wondering where in the hell Alessa and Adriano were at the moment.

"I can't miss this trip," Adriano murmured, keeping his tone low as to keep anyone else from overhearing their conversation. "*I* made this damn deal, Lissa."

She held their kids tighter as he met her gaze, and the worry he was feeling reflected back in his stare. Always the youngest, she thought. Still, in his business, Adriano was the youngest made man in the Outfit who always felt a need to prove himself. Not that anyone ever went out of their way to make him feel like a rookie or some shit, but he felt that way all the time. Like he had to make sure everyone and anyone around him knew that despite his age, he still had all the capabilities and experience that mattered to make money, and get the job done.

This trip to the Maldives for Christmas was just another one of those things. Oh, sure, they were going to have fun. It was a vacation, too. They'd spend the holidays together with their friends, and business would barely touch the women and kids, if at all. Maybe in passing if someone felt like letting them know what had gone on.

But that was it.

Still, there would be business. A whole arms deal Adriano had set up himself through contacts he'd pulled together. Tommas's effort to increase his presence in trafficking guns fell to whoever was able to pull a deal together, and get their hands on the weapons.

Theo got the weapons.

Adriano made the deal.

So yeah, he kind of had to be on that plane. He had to make it to the Maldives, and be there to speak because *he* was the one who made that damn deal.

Suddenly, for no particular reason, Corrine burst into howling, wailing tears next to her mother's side. Alessa let out a loud sigh, and side-eyed her husband before trying to console their daughter.

It took the woman behind the counter another ten minutes—all the while, Corrine wailed—to finally get the tickets through.

But they came through.

"Let's hope security doesn't take forever," Adriano said, scooping a still-crying Corrine into his arms. "Or we're screwed, Lissa."

She laughed.

Of course, security would take forever.

Life was having a good laugh at them today.

THREE

Abriella and Tommas

ABRIELLA

"Where are Alessa and Adriano?" Theo asked as he kept his two-year-old nephew occupied by pulling on the leather cord around his neck. "Hey, be easy, Cory."

The boy beamed up at his uncle, and yanked on the leather cord again.

Theo gave the toddler a look.

The toddler *looked* right back.

"You're impossible," Theo told the boy.

Cory let out a loud squealing laugh because to him, this shit was funny. He lived for this nonsense with his uncle. No one else let him get away with as much crap as Theo did when it came right down to it.

"Just like your father," Theo added.

"No, he is not," Damian—Cory's father—said absently as he cleaned a mess off the front of his other son's shirt. Chocolate, or something. Kids were always getting into *everything.* It was impossible to keep them clean for a spread of a couple of hours. "He's just like you, Theo. He doesn't get that shit from me or Lily."

"Accurate," Lily said, glancing away from the windows overlooking the plane that was taxing up to the gate. "*You're* the bad influence, Theo. Don't even try to deny it."

Theo looked like someone had just smacked him in the face with a shovel before he made a noise under his breath. "Listen, it's not *pick on Theo day*, okay. Find someone else to bother." He patted Cory on the top of his head. "He's just fine the way he is, even if he does get it from me."

If it were any other time or day or fuck, even *place*, Abriella might have laughed. No, she definitely would have laughed, and then promptly pointed out that Theo asked for all of this. From Cory's behavior, to the way everyone liked to point this shit out to him. But it wasn't any other day, and she was just about done with this damn day.

"Did you text Adriano?" Theo asked Tommas.

Tommas nodded as he took his son from his wife's outstretched arms. Tommaso squirmed, unhappy that he was being passed on to yet someone else's arms instead of being put down on the floor so that he could run and play. All the energy in the world, but Abriella didn't know where her son got it from. God knew she had a hard time keeping up some days.

"No!" the two-year-old shouted.

"Almost on the plane," Tommas told their son.

There was nothing Tommaso liked more than flying. But even the promise of getting on the plane soon was not enough to make the toddler happy.

Abriella sighed. "This was a bad idea. We should have flown privately, or—"

"Kind of late now," Theo muttered.

At least, Abriella thought, Theo was finally understanding why this hadn't been one of his and Eve's greatest ideas. Not that Abriella felt the need to point that out any more than it already had been over the course of the morning.

The kids were doing that well enough on their own, frankly. It only took one of the toddlers to start acting up for all the rest of them to follow suit.

"Oh, good, we didn't miss the fucking plane," a familiar voice grumbled behind Abriella. "What a whole damn mess this day is."

She spun around on her heels to find Adriano and Alessa approaching with their two girls. One in their father's arms, and the other in their mother's. At the moment, Alessa and Adriano looked about like the rest of them did.

Exhausted.

Over it.

On their last freaking rope.

"Don't cuss," Alessa said, rolling her eyes.

Adriano scowled. "Today is the day for all the swearing, Lissa."

"Yes, but—"

Adriano bent down to let the oldest of their two girls on the floor. The second Corrine's feet touched the ground, she darted forward and stole the toy Joe had been quietly playing with while sitting in his chair beside his mother and father.

The quietest kid of the bunch, right there. Joe was the easiest of all their large brood to please, and make sure he stayed out of trouble. Being the oldest of all the kids, that was also a great help when it came right down to it.

Unless, of course, someone interrupted him or took away his things. Then, Joe turned into every other three-year-old who was ready to break some shit and make a lot of noise.

Like right now.

"My *truck*!" Joe wailed. "Gives back my truck!"

It was like a domino effect, really. One kid started to cry, and then slowly—one after another like a fucking train wreck you couldn't stop and you just had to watch happen all the while—another kid started crying, too. And then another, and another.

There was no stopping it.

Nothing could be done.

Tommas and Abriella stood side by side and stared helplessly at one another as even their own son started wailing at their feet. Tommaso looked up at them with the biggest eyes—confusion and unhappiness staring back—as fat tears slid down his cheeks.

Life with toddlers was not for the weak.

Nope.

"I love you, Tommy," Abriella murmured, "you know that, right?"

Tommas nodded. "Yeah, babe."

"Good, so then you won't mind me telling you that if you *don't* fix this shit somehow, I cannot guarantee how much longer that love is going to last."

Abriella knew her husband wouldn't even take that personally. She was mostly joking, even if she was serious about the wanting him to fix this whole thing. And no wonder …

They were drawing attention. People waiting at the gate to get on the same plane were now staring at them, and their large group. Eyeing the kids like little bugs they thought were probably going to ruin their flight.

Not that they would be wrong.

Tommas scooped their son up from the ground, and held the boy tightly as he headed for the woman waiting behind a desk at the gate. Abriella followed behind him just because she felt like doing something other than listen to kids scream for another ten minutes. God knew it would take at least that long to get them all calmed down again.

"Thirteen seats just opened up if you had people on a wait list, thanks," Tommas said.

The woman's eyes widened. "I beg your—"

"We're not flying today."

"Oh, we're going home?" Abriella asked him.

Tommas gave her a look from the side, grinned, and leaned forward to catch her mouth with his own like nothing was wrong in his world. Like the kids weren't all melting down around them, and she didn't have a raging headache.

"We're not flying on *this* flight," he told her. "I have something better in mind. What do I always tell you about trips, huh?"

Abriella grinned. "Always have a backup plan."

"That's right, babe."

It paid to be rich, really.

FOUR

Eve and Theo

EVE

Evelina had never really been a fan of flying. And then once, Theo had taken her out in a small single-engine plane after earning his pilot's license, and suddenly, she was forced to face that fear head-on. Not that her husband would have made her go out in the plane with him if she was scared, because he wasn't the type.

But she had wanted to go. She'd wanted so badly to celebrate that moment with him, so she swallowed her fear, and got in the damn plane.

The first ten minutes had been absolutely terrifying. She still remembered how her heart had felt as they climbed higher in that plane. Like if it didn't stop beating altogether, then it was going to race right out of her chest. But that was the thing about Theo, too. Eve swore the man just knew when she was scared. Like he could feel her fear, or something.

He'd started speaking, his voice echoing through the comms in her ears as the plane leveled out. Soon enough, they'd been in the air for twenty minutes, and Eve was distracted from listening to Theo talk to her as she stared at the beautiful sights below her.

She didn't mind flying so much after that.

"Not really all that surprised that Tommas had a private jet on stand-by," Theo murmured beside her. Sitting in the aisle seat so that she could take the window, he had a better view than she did of the rest of the people on the jet. "Although, he could have saved us a lot of trouble today and just directed us there instead."

Eve laughed as Theo's hand curved around her thigh under her dress. "I think the point of today was Tommas pointing out we don't always have the *best* ideas when it comes to the kids … or I guess, traveling with all of them."

Theo made a noise under his breath. "That's fair."

It wasn't a lie. They were the only ones in their large group of friends that still, after all this time, were childless. Not that they didn't enjoy children because they did. They were always the first ones to speak up and take anybody's kids when they needed a night away. They had three extra bedrooms in their house saved just for their nieces and nephews to use that were filled with toys and things the kids loved.

They just … never wanted their own.

Eve had wondered over time if that might change for them. She waited for that motherly urge to strike that would remind her of the ovaries in her body that had a fucking time clock ticking down.

It never came.

She just didn't feel the urge to have her own biological children, and she was fine with that. Theo never said anything one way or the other. He had the grandest time taking care of everyone else's kids, and being the terrible influence that he was.

Whether he wanted to admit it or not, he owned that shit.

The *fun* uncle.

"Or maybe the lesson was that we shouldn't all travel with five kids," Theo said. "Maybe we should just wait until they're older. At least then, they'll actually remember these trips."

Eve made a face. "No—private flights, instead."

Theo chuckled. "Yeah, all right."

Because yeah, despite the fact she didn't want her own kids, she still wanted everybody else's kids around her. That made her happy.

At least, she didn't get as defensive anymore when someone else thought to look at her and outright ask, "When are you going to have one?"

Sure, it was invasive. Like their private business or choices was public consumption simply because someone dared to ask about it. But she didn't get as offended as she used to, and she knew people didn't really mean any harm when they asked.

Thing was—Eve figured that wasn't her purpose, or Theo's. They weren't put on the earth, or given each other, simply to procreate and bring life to the next generation of their family. They had other things to do. A different purpose, even if they hadn't quite figured out what that was just yet.

"Hey," Theo murmured.

Eve glanced over at him. He was grinning in that way of his. A way that told her he was thinking of something fun or bad or a mixture of the two. That had never changed where her husband was concerned.

"What?" she asked.

"Let's go explore. They're all passed out. I want to check out this plane."

Eve arched a brow. "It's a private jet. You've seen one, you've seen them all."

"But not *this* one, Eve. Come on."

Theo didn't give her the chance to argue further. Instead, he tugged her up from the seat, finally allowing Eve a view of the rest of their gang on the plane. Sure enough, it looked like everyone else had finally calmed down, and were all asleep. Even the parents.

"Long day," she said.

Theo smirked. "It ain't over, babe."

"What?"

What was he planning?

Theo was always planning *something.*

He tugged her along the wide aisle of the private jet until they were at the very back of the plane. Bypassing a sizeable bathroom—for a plane—he pushed open a door at the end that opened up to what looked to be a small office with a double bed against port windows.

Right then, Eve knew.

Knew what he was planning.

Knew why he was smirking.

Fucking man.

Theo closed the door, and didn't even give Eve the chance to speak before he flicked the lock, and grabbed her. Those hands of his slipped under her dress as his lips attacked hers. A burning, harsh kiss that drove her crazy and took her breath away at the same time. He backed her into the door as he worked on getting her dress higher, never once breaking their kiss.

It was only once her dress was up around her hips that he finally pulled away from the kiss just long enough to wrap his hands around the waistband of her panties, and then yank them down her legs.

"Theo!"

"Hush," he muttered, kneeling down to kiss a path across her pubic bone. "Don't want to wake up the rest of them, do we? Then, this ends, Eve. Figure it *out*."

"You're an ass—"

Theo glanced up. "An asshole about to fuck you twenty thousand feet in the air, yeah."

Well …

"Yeah, that sounds good," Eve admitted.

Theo just laughed again.

It took him no time at all to shed the rest of the clothes between them, and then get Eve on her back on the double bed. She barely even felt the turbulence of the flight once Theo was between her thighs, and finding home.

He went slow at first—teasing and tempting her. Promising wicked things as he filled her full, and then drew out slow enough to make her want to scream.

Except she couldn't be too loud, so she settled on hooking her legs around his waist, and holding him tight to her body to make her point clear. All she cared about was the way his mouth felt on her throat while he fucked her, and just how good his hands felt tugging on her hair as he murmured all those dirty words.

Yeah, damn.

God, she loved this man.

Bad influences and all.

FIVE

Lily and Damian

DAMIAN

No shame, and all, but Damian had learned over the years that having kids was nothing more than a battle of the survival of the fittest. If someone was stupid enough to give kids an inch, the kids didn't just take a mile when they ran with it, no. They took *ten*, and laughed the whole way like you should have known better.

And you should have.

Even knowing this, Damian had somehow convinced himself that it would be a good idea to put his kids on a plane, fly them to a whole other country for the holidays, and everything would be just fine. Because that's also what kids did to you—they made you fucking delusional.

"Slow down, Cory!"

His youngest son glanced back at his father down the boardwalk connecting the vacation huts spread across the scenic spot. Each hut was suspended over the water—glittering, crystal blue water that was as clear as the sky above their heads. The Maldives really were quite a fucking place. Beautiful, and peaceful. This particular spot where they had all chosen to spend their vacation was a well-known resort, although more expensive, and far more private.

All things Damian liked.

He still couldn't have his son running *that far* ahead of him, though. Especially given the fact Cory, far more than Joe, really, found trouble like nobody understood. All it took was someone looking away from that kid for a second too long, and he was gone. They couldn't afford for their kid to find trouble here.

Too much fucking water.

"Cory!"

Damian dropped his oldest son's hand, but Lily was quick to grab it before he darted ahead. Cory had only really skipped ahead about ten feet, but it didn't matter. It still made Damian nervous. People didn't understand that drowning was a silent fucking death. Especially in children. They didn't shout and flail … they just slipped under before you even noticed it was happening.

He could tell already—given how fucking paranoid his thoughts were—that most of this vacation would be spent with him in a panic about his sons, and keeping them away from the water, or the boardwalk …. or doorways considering their huts were right over top of the goddamn water.

Once he caught Cory around his little waist, he didn't really scold the boy. He just threw him over his shoulder like Cory was a sack of potatoes, and turned around to wait for his wife to catch up. Lily, still smiling sweetly and as pretty as ever even after a long flight where she barely slept at all, gave him a sigh.

"Keep a hold of him," she said, "we're almost there anyway."

"There better be locks on the door, or I am fucking killing Theo," he muttered.

Joe looked up at his father, and in all his three-year-old wisdom, said, "Can't kills Uncle Theo. He's *family*."

Lily smiled again.

Damian sighed that time.

He patted his oldest boy on the top of his head with the hand that wasn't locked around a kicking and giggling Cory. "Yeah, that's right, little man."

Joe nodded, still holding tight to his mother's hand. Quiet and a loner, the kid was easy to please and almost always followed the rules as long as people were willing to give him his space. Everyone liked to say that Joe reminded them of Damian. That his moods and demeanor, even at his age, reflected his father's in a lot of ways.

Damian didn't always know that it was true.

Sometimes, Joe reminded Damian of someone else entirely.

His uncle—Dino.

But that was a discussion for another day, and today was not that day. This was supposed to be a happy trip—relaxing for the girls, fun for the kids, and a mix of the two for the guys, even if they did have a bit of work involved while they were here. It wasn't the time to be bringing up old wounds, even if they were mostly healed.

"All right," Lily said, peering down the way, "I think that's ours right there."

Further down the opposite way, Damian watched as Tommas and Abriella slipped inside their hut with Tommaso hanging over his father's shoulder. Alessa and Adriano were closest to them, while Theo and Eve's place was closest to Damian and Lily. But really, they were maybe a couple of minutes apart walking distance.

"You got the keys?" Damian asked, following behind his wife while still holding Cory tight. He was really going to have to have a conversation with that kid about safety while they were there, although he didn't know how much good it would do them. Lily flashed the keys over her shoulder, causing them to jingle at the same time. "Good, let's get these monsters inside the safety of four goddamn walls."

"Language," his wife murmured.

Damian just rolled his eyes.

Lily had the right hut, although … he didn't know if that was an accurate description for the place when she unlocked the door, and they stepped inside. Oh, sure, from the outside it resembled something of a hut suspended over the water, but inside was something else entirely. The walls facing the front were solid, and private. But a good portion of the walls facing the water were made of glass, including two sliding doors that led to a hot tub in the back, and a deck to lounge on, or jump off to swim in the crystal clear water. Modern furniture, hardwood floors, and rooms that … well, weren't really rooms.

The sections were mostly made into rooms by sheer fabric hanging down to separate them, but it looked like there were darker curtains at the ends to pull too to make it less see through.

An inverted section of the floor was covered in large white pillows—a sitting area. The kitchen was small, but the dining area was large enough for all of them to eat, plus have the others come over, likely. A woven, bright colored hammock hung in front of a section of windows overlooking the ocean. Damian never did understand the appeal of hammocks, he always felt like he was going to fall right out of one. But to each their own, he supposed.

All in all, it was beautiful.

And comfortable.

"And not kid friendly," Damian muttered to himself.

He put Cory to the floor, a little less worried than he had been outside. At least he could see practically everything but inside the bathroom, so it wasn't like his son could get too far before his father would find him or catch up to him.

Lily glanced back at him after she had let Joe go. "Tommas said they put in those requests for all the safety gates and locks, right?"

They had.

"Supposed to be under the sink in the kitchen, from what I understand," Damian said.

"Well, once we get all that up, it'll be better."

"Slightly," he corrected his wife. "It will be slightly better."

"Damian—"

"This much water makes me nervous, Lily."

"Yeah, I know."

He'd had an incident as a kid—almost drowned when he fell off the end of a dock when the adults weren't paying attention. Not that anybody had ever paid any attention to Damian when he was younger. Fact was, he'd never learned to swim until he was a teenager, but that almost-drowning when he was ten stuck with him.

Damian blinked, and Lily was standing right in front of him. Her soft hands came up to cup his face, and like this, he had no choice but to stare at her. Only her. Not the water, or the unlocked doors. He didn't have time to go inside his head and wallow in his currently unfounded fears because his wife was looking at him, and everything was always better—no excuses or exceptions—when Lily was looking at him. Dragging in a hard breath, Damian offered her a smile.

She smiled back, then leaned in and kissed him on the mouth. "It's fine, Damian. It'll be fine."

"Yeah, I know."

"But we'll be safe, take extra precautions …"

"I'm going around to lock everybody else's fucking shit up, too."

His wife nodded. "Okay."

"Ow, Cory, don't hit!"

"I nots!"

Lily turned around, giving Damian a good view of their two sons. Apparently, Joe had climbed into the hammock to lay down, and then must have helped his brother inside as well. Except the two were now fighting again, smacking each other and making the hammock rock dangerously.

Story of his life with those two. He doubted that was ever going to change.

SIX

Alessa and Adriano

ADRIANO

Out of the corner of his eye, Adriano watched Alessa breastfeed Lissa as he continued his phone call. He'd much rather climb in the bed with his wife amongst white pillows and soft sheets, but business never ended, and he needed to take care of this first before he could get on with the rest of his day.

A few feet away from the bed, Corrine slept happily in her portable playpen. Those things were a bitch to travel with, and yet, it had proved more than worth it to bring it along, too.

"You do understand, Mr. Conti, that should this not go as we had planned—"

"Then, what?" Adriano asked, trying to keep his tone cool and not too sharp. Not that the man on the other end of the call even proved he deserved Adriano's respect at the moment, but he didn't want this entire fucking thing to be a wasted trip just because someone decided to catch a goddamn attitude. "If things do not go as planned, and we can't work out a deal on the cache of weapons, then I will tell you exactly what will happen, Mr. Torres."

"And what is that, exactly?" the man asked gruffly.

"We will go our separate ways. *We* will find someone else to sell the weapons to, and *you* will find someone else to buy from. Of course, that means more time you go without the artillery you claim to need for your little … rebellion."

Yes, that was a good way to put the fact that this man was working to overthrow his government with a large mass of people. That's what the fucking media would call it when the uprising really got started.

"I thought we agreed—"

"Yes, yes. Not to talk about that." Adriano sighed, scrubbed a hand down his face, and glanced at his wife again. Instead of focusing on little Lissa, the second—who everyone kept saying was too old for her to breastfeed now—Alessa was watching him. A line of worry creased her brow. That bothered him. She didn't need to worry at all, but especially not about this trip. She probably couldn't help it, though. So was their life. "Listen, you keep up your end, and we will keep up our end, Mr. Torres. You need something, and we have what you want. It's as simple as that."

The phone turned silent for a moment. Adriano almost wondered if the man had hung up the phone on him, but then the man's voice filtered through again, proving that was not the case.

"And negotiations are possible on certain things?"

Adriano smiled a bit. "Negotiations are welcomed, but keep in mind, we aren't here to support or help your cause. We are here to make *money*. If you believe appealing to our sympathetic sides about your cause will get those weapons into your hands at a cheaper cost, I can promise you will be wasting your breath."

Another beat of silence passed before the man muttered, "Fine. I suppose the next time we speak will be face to face at the meeting, yes?"

"That is the plan, Mr. Torres."

"I look forward to it, Mr. Conti."

Adriano hung up the call, and immediately dialed another familiar number. Alessa shot him a look as if to ask, *What are you doing now*? He elected to ignore his wife for a second. Call him paranoid, but Adriano never liked it when people became *too* demanding. There was something about that which put him on edge.

The very last place he needed to be, honestly.

"Adriano?" Mikey asked when he picked up the call on the third ring. "What can I do for you? I thought you were supposed to be enjoying your vacation with the rest of them?"

"I am enjoying my vacation like everyone else is, thanks."

"Well, what can I do for you?"

"Nothing too big, … just move the cache again. Say, to the other side of the city. They're already packed in trucks, so it shouldn't be too difficult to move them to a new location, should it?"

Mikey was quiet before he muttered, "That's *four trucks* of guns, Adriano."

Yeah, but part of their earlier deal with Mr. Torres was a sneak peek at the weapons. He'd sent a man into Chicago, and while they had done their best to hide where they were keeping the weapons stored, it was very possible that somehow, the man figured out an approximate area of their location.

He didn't have any reason to think that was the case, or that the buyer might try to steal their cache instead of buying … but he kept going back to the fact that he didn't like people who made demands, and paranoia was a bitch. Like fuck was he going to do all this work for someone to come along and *steal* the weapons just because they had a bright idea.

"Doesn't matter," Adriano countered, "move the cache."

Mikey sighed hard. "Fine. You want an update when they reach the new point?"

"Of course."

"Will do, Adriano."

Mikey didn't even bother to say goodbye, instead hanging up the phone without any warning. Adriano didn't even mind. He had other things to focus on now like making sure this meeting went off without a hitch, and business was *good.* He glanced at his phone again, ready to make another phone call, but Alessa's voice stopped him.

"Will you put that down?"

He glanced his wife's way. She smoothed her palm over Lissa's head, and tipped her head toward the empty side of the bed as if to silently ask him to come lay with her.

"I'm trying—"

"I know exactly what you are trying to do, Adriano," Alessa said, "and I still think you can relax for five minutes, put the phone away, and forget about it for the moment."

"Lissa—"

"It's going to be fine, Adriano."

She was so sure.

So calm.

Probably right, too.

Adriano chuckled. "I'm just on edge, I think."

"I know."

It felt like, even after all this time as a made man, he was still the youngest person who held his rank amongst many. He still had to prove himself constantly. He tried not to let it bother him, but it was almost impossible to do, too.

"Come here," Alessa murmured.

Well, he supposed the phone calls *could* wait. Slipping the phone inside his pocket, he climbed onto the bed with his wife. His mind drifted back to the guns and the deal and the possible problems … and then quickly drifted back to his wife when she chattered on beside him.

That was the thing about his wife—she spoke, he listened. Things were easier that way, and simpler. They had fewer battles when he just chose to shut up and listen instead of trying to talk over her. Being married so young had probably been a mark against them in a way, although they would never willingly admit it. Things hadn't been easy when they were technically still two selfish kids who didn't know the first thing about enduring love or being married.

They figured it out, though.

Here they were.

Happy wife, happy life.

"Love you, Adriano," she said.

He reached up to stroke her cheek. "Love you, Lissa."

SEVEN

Eve and Theo

THEO

"For the record, Eve," Theo grumbled, trailing behind his wife by a couple of feet on the docks that separated each vacation hut, "this is *way too early* for any-fucking-body to be awake. Look, the sun isn't even up."

He wasn't lying, and it was *way too early.* Theo didn't roll his ass out of bed before ten for anything less than his boss, his wife's pussy, or a hell of a lot of money. Technically, none of those things were actually on the table at the moment unless …

"Are we gonna go fuck in the water?" he asked. "Because I am up for that, Eve."

She shot him a look over her shoulder, all sweet smiles and twinkling eyes. He knew her answer before she even said it simply because if she was planning something dirty, that smile of hers would be a whole lot more sinful.

Damn.

"Will you quit whining?"

"It's six in the morning," Theo groaned. "What part of the fact that I can't actually function at six in the morning don't you understand, *donna*? You're killing me here, Eve. *Killing me.* You're going to give me a heart attack from the stress of forcing me to get up this early. And on a vacation, no less."

It didn't fail to amaze him how years ago, Theo stayed up for hours on end just to keep from falling asleep as much as possible. The nightmares had still been an awful bitch back then, to be fair. Over the years, he found sleep came easier for him, but especially when he was sharing a bed with Eve.

He still had the nightmares occasionally, but they were fewer and far between, now. They weren't as traumatic when he did have them, either. He came out of them easier, and recovered far faster when one did creep up on him. He didn't fear sleep anymore. Actually, he kind of fucking loved it.

Which was why he shouldn't be up right now.

"Do you want a bow to go in your hair, too?"

"What?"

"You sound like you started your period."

Christ.

He loved his wife. She was sharp and quick in ways a lot of people except him didn't get to see. She saved all that wit for him when he was giving her shit, and she knew she had to give it back just as hard.

Theo snapped his mouth shut, but not before murmuring, "I'm just saying that fucking in the water would have made waking up this early much more worth it."

"If you shut up, you might get that later."

Yep.

He shut right up.

All the way up.

Zipped lips all the way.

"Besides," Eve continued, coming closer to Adriano and Alessa's hut, "you know everybody with kids are already awake and getting ready for the day. They're always waiting on your lazy ass because you don't have kids, and you like to sleep in."

"I take their kids all the time!"

"Don't yell. Now be good and help me get the kids back to our place."

Theo shot her a look, but Eve pretended like she didn't even see it. "Are you going to watch them all by yourself for the entire day, or …? Because I am not going to be here."

"Quite aware, and no. Just for the morning. I got all that stuff for pancakes, remember? You put the locks on everything because Damian was going insane about it."

"Well, he did have a point."

Not that Theo was willing to admit that to his brother-in-law. If he gave Damian an inch, the man took a fucking mile. So was their way, really.

Eve knocked on the front door of the hut, and stepped back. Adriano swung the door open less than two seconds later. Theo had to laugh at the fact the man already had both kids ready, and a bag for each one. It was a little past six in the fucking morning, and he looked like he had been up for a couple of hours.

Eve took baby Lissa.

Corrine ran out to grab Theo's hand.

Adriano pointed a finger at Eve, saying, "I don't know what you women have planned today, but my wife has been telling me to mind my goddamn business all last night. It better be worth it."

Eve smirked. "We'll see, won't we?"

In the doorway, Adriano's gaze narrowed before he shot Theo a look, shook his head, and then closed the door. Without a word, Eve continued down the path to the next hut. Theo trailed behind her like he had before, but this time, with Corrine bouncing beside him and tugging on his hand the whole way. The little one never stopped talking, and he swore she said twenty words for every single step she took, too.

Kids were cute like that, really.

And busy.

Little monsters.

At the next hut, Tommas and Abriella's, Eve knocked on the door a hell of a lot quieter than she had for Alessa and Adriano's place. Theo didn't wonder why for very long when Tommas was quick to open the door with a half-sleeping Tommaso slung over his shoulder. He already had a finger pressed to his lips.

"Don't say a word—Ella is still sleeping. I want her to fucking stay that way. You just take him, and go. Got it?"

Eve laughed quietly, gesturing for Theo to come forward and take the tired toddler. "You got it."

Somehow, he managed to balance holding Tommaso and keeping a grip on Corrine's hand at the same time. Tommaso's sleepiness only lasted as long as it took for Corrine's chattiness to start back up again, but they were almost to the far end where Damian and Lily's hut was situated when the kids really started getting loud again.

Thing was, they didn't even have to knock on the front door of the last place. Damian was already outside with Cory on one side of him, and Joe playing with a truck in the hammock in the front sitting area.

Damian shrugged when Theo asked, "Up early, or what?"

"Kids, man."

Yeah, kids explained *everything*.

Cory darted forward, and Tommaso finally wanted to be let down to play with his cousin. Theo's shoulder thanked the heavy toddler for giving it a break.

"Are you coming with aunt Eve today, Joe?" his wife called to the quietest of all the kids.

Joe made a face, glanced between his father and aunt, and then shrugged. "I guess."

Eve laughed, and met Theo's gaze over her shoulder. "He really knows how to stroke someone's ego, doesn't he?"

That was little Joe.

"You ready to get a start on this day, or what?" Damian asked Theo.

"More like, is Adriano and Tommas?"

Damian chuckled. "Truth."

Eve worked on getting Joe out of the hammock, and convincing him *nobody* was going to take his truck while he spent the morning with her. And didn't he like pancakes? Yes, he did.

"Theo, stop gossiping like a teenage girl and help me get all the kids back to our place."

Theo rolled his eyes, and ignored Damian's laughter following him as he headed after his wife. "What are you planning to do today, anyway?"

"Well, it's not just me. *All* the girls are going to do something. Won't be the same when you get back."

His brow knotted. "I don't understand."

"That's the point. Besides, it's Christmas Eve. Do better, Theo."

Damn woman.

Good thing he loved her.

EIGHT

Abriella and Tommas

TOMMAS

Tommas no sooner had the door to the vacation hut shut, and he was already heading across the open floor to head for where his wife was still happily sleeping behind sheer curtains. If there was anything he disliked about this vacation spot, it was the fact that inside the huts, there was very little privacy from the children.

Which meant he wasn't getting to love his wife nearly as much as he needed and wanted to. But he had—at most—one hour to spend with his wife before the guys would be waiting outside to head on their … business portion of this vacation, and he planned on using every single one of those minutes to his advantage.

He doubted Abriella was going to complain, honestly.

Tommas wasted no fucking time stripping out of the night clothes he'd pulled on the evening before. By the time he was on his side of the bed, he was already naked and *hard.* So was his life with this woman sleeping unaware on the bed. He went to sleep rock hard, and woke up with a steel rod every fucking morning. He got turned on simply by watching his wife doing laundry. If it weren't for responsibilities and life getting in the way, he'd keep his wife in bed all the damn time.

He was so weak.

Pussy weak.

Sliding into the bed next to his wife, Tommas didn't even bother to try and wake Abriella up slowly. In nothing but a silk nightie that barely covered her bare ass, the only thing he really wanted to do was get his hands and lips on her body. So, he did just that.

His hands pushed her nightie high while his lips found her throat first. He knew the second she woke up from the way her pulse picked up under the nip of his teeth. Her soft gasp echoed into the room, filling him up with a lust like nothing else. He kept kissing her even as her murmurings filtered through his senses.

"What are you … *oh*," she breathed.

He dotted kisses down her throat, and over the toned expanse of her stomach after he'd pushed her nightie high enough to free her skin to his mouth. He loved the taste of his wife first thing in the morning. It was just about as good as how she tasted after sex, really. Like sweetness and salt—uniquely her with a touch of him.

Because God knew he was all over her.

Constantly.

Like an animal urge he just couldn't fucking kick no matter what he did. Every single person needed to know this woman was his, and he didn't forget to remind anyone who might have thought differently.

"Jesus Christ, Tommy."

Her words were high, and airless.

The way he liked them best, really.

He planned on getting them far louder when he got his head buried between her thighs. Abriella knew it was coming; he could feel it in the clench of her stomach when his tongue traced her navel, and the way her hips lifted to press against him. Her fingers threaded into his hair and tugged hard enough to make his scalp sting when he finally slipped between her thighs properly.

His mouth found her sex, and Tommas was done for. Harder than granite, and grinding against the bed as he ate the heaven between his wife's thighs. There was nothing easy or sweet about the way his tongue lashed at Abriella's clit again and again. It wasn't like she cared for soft and sweet, anyway.

She wanted to come. Each stroke of his tongue and the harsh way his fingers dug into her inner thighs to keep her thighs from locking around his head had her back arching off the bed, and her cries rising impossibly higher.

Sweet Jesus.

He adored his name in his wife's mouth.

Pleading.

Loud.

Perfect, really.

"Oh, my God, Tommy, *please* …"

It was only once he drew her throbbing slit between his lips, and sucked hard that she finally came undone on the bed. Those fingernails of hers dragged through his hair as she tensed all over, and a shout left her lips that echoed in the quiet hut. Her trembling rocked them both, and for a second he enjoyed the sight of his wife as she panted her way through her first orgasm of the morning. If he had his way—and he would because he always did—it would be the first of fucking *many*.

Tommas didn't give Abriella time to recover before he was sliding back up her body, leaving hot kisses that tasted like her come in his wake. Her gaze locked on his as her heavy breaths began to even out, and she graced him with one of her wicked smiles when his fingers wrapped around her throat right under her jaw. Pushing her head back into the pillow, he dropped a kiss to her lips that seared him from the inside out. There was something about the way his wife's lips worked against his, how her tongue darted in and out of his mouth to get as much of her taste as she could from his lips that drove him crazy.

Her thighs wrapped around him in an instant, dragging him in close enough that she could grind her wet pussy against his length. And when her hand slipped between their bodies to get the head of his dick pressing against her slit, the world tilted back on its axis again. He thrust home, and life was good again.

Beautiful again.

Just like he needed.

Nothing could make his stress and worries disappear quite like fucking his wife did. Nothing could make him forget about *everything* like being nine inches deep inside Abriella.

"Please tell me Tommaso is—"

"Gone for the morning. Rise and shine, wife."

Abriella laughed breathlessly. "I figured."

"I didn't think you'd mind this, actually."

"Perfect way to wake up," his wife groaned. "Thank you."

Tommas dragged himself out of her body until just the head of his cock was stretching her open, and then he was pushing back in again. Harder the second time—enough to make his wife suck in a ragged breath as her eyes fluttered shut. She was quite a sight underneath him, her lashes fanning her pinked cheeks, and her hair a mess against the pillows.

He dropped a soft kiss to her lips, and tightened his fingers at her throat. "What do you want, huh? Tell me, baby, and I'll give it to you."

"Just fuck me, Tommas."

Yeah, that's all he wanted, too.

He did just that.

Tommas didn't make it out of the hut within the hour like he was supposed to, certainly not dressed and ready for his day trip for business with the guys, anyway. He didn't crawl away from his wife until his phone started buzzing and buzzing. He figured whichever man it was calling him—probably Damian, but it could have been Adriano, too—wasn't going to fucking give up until he showed his face.

He had just finished buttoning up the silk dress shirt he wore as he stepped outside of the hut. His suit jacket was tossed over his arm, and his watch wasn't even fucking clasped, but his morning had been spent well, and that was all that mattered to Tommas.

"Really?" Damian asked where he stood waiting with Theo and Adriano just a few steps away from the front door. "You're not even dressed yet?"

"Be lucky I came out at all. I could have spent my whole goddamn afternoon doing exactly what I was doing which would be far better than sitting in a car with you three for two hours. I don't have to go at all today, remember?"

Adriano scowled. "Show of faith, yeah?"

Theo rolled his eyes, and turned to head down the docks. "Listen, nobody likes to be woken up at six in the morning *or* dragged away from their wife's pussy, but here we are. So let's all shut up, and get this done so we can get back to sleeping, fucking, and whatever else we want to do on this vacation. Also, as my wife told me this morning, it's Christmas Eve, and nobody wants to deal with anybody's shit on Christmas Eve, so cut it out."

Theo DeLuca, everyone.

Always the voice of reason.

NINE

Alessa and Adriano

ADRIANO

"And you talked to the buyer again, correct?"

Adriano nodded. "Several times, Tommas."

"We don't expect issues, right?"

Usually, Adriano would bristle a bit about people questioning him when he'd already repeated the same shit over and over again. But this was Tommas, and he figured his boss was just as edgy about this transaction as the rest of them, frankly. Not because he expected it to go wrong, but rather, because he wanted everything to go right.

As Theo had told Adriano months ago when he first brought up this idea, the Maldives deal would officially be their *first* foray into the gun trafficking business. And in this business, it was all about being able to deliver without trouble, and keeping a good reputation. That was how more contracts came up, and buyers continued to shell out money for guns.

If their first contract went bad, that wasn't going to do anything good for their reputations in this line of work. It was unlikely they would be able to sell the cache of weapons they had stumbled upon, and stole which meant they would have a whole warehouse full of useless guns sitting there costing them money.

They all needed this to go well.

Including the buyer …

Speaking of which, Adriano turned to Tommas again, saying, "I don't expect any issues. Honestly, I think he's as eager to get this started as we are."

He didn't mention the buyer had gotten a bit demanding the last time they spoke for more than two minutes. Besides, that would only serve to piss Tommas off, and it was never good to take Tommas into a meeting angry. Absolutely fucking nobody won when Tommas was pissed and ready to teach someone a lesson.

"I did have the weapons moved again," Adriano mentioned offhandedly.

"Why?"

"As a precaution."

It wasn't entirely a lie, and it would keep Tommas happy. Both good things, Adriano decided.

"All right." Tommas glanced down at his watch, and then back up again, only this time he was staring forward into the front seats where Damian was driving, and Theo was fiddling with the radio. "How much longer, Damian?"

"Not very. A few more minutes to the hotel, I think. You know, as long as this fucking GPS is correct."

"This was too long of a drive. I hate sitting for this long."

"You picked the hotel," Theo countered his boss from the front. "You wanted it far enough from our vacation spot that there was no chance of them following us back or finding us ahead of time, remember?"

Tommas rolled his eyes, stared out the window, and grunted, "I remember just fine why I picked the place, thank you."

Damian wasn't wrong, and the GPS had been correct. It was another ten minutes of driving, and listening to Theo's terrible fucking screaming music before the resort hotel Tommas had chosen for the meeting came into view. Once in front of the place, a valet came up to the vehicle to take the car while the four men stepped out of the vehicle. Adriano was already regretting his choice to wear a silk dress shirt considering it practically clung to his damp skin the second he was standing in the heat.

Theo headed inside first, as they had previously agreed, to check on their reservations and to see if their guest had already arrived. They were supposed to show up first, and then the buyer. If the guy couldn't follow very basic instructions, then chances were, the rest of this would already be doomed to fucking fail.

"A table is ready in the dining room," Theo said, coming out from the front of the hotel. "They've got it all set up for us. The buyer hasn't arrived yet, but they expect him within the next fifteen or so minutes. So, whenever you are ready, Tommy."

"Great," Tommas said. "Let's get this started, then."

Adriano didn't pay very much attention to the inside of the hotel or the grand entryway when they entered the place. They had already staked the place out online, and had someone go in and take pictures to send to them as a *just in case.* It was always good to plan for things ahead of time, and none of them were the type of men to leave shit to chance.

Once directed into the hotel's dining area, they were situated in a small private section with large windows overlooking swaying trees and a rather scenic view of the water in the distance. The four of them kept their conversation quiet and entirely off the topic of the business at hand as servers came in with menus, coffee, and water.

They didn't order anything more than the coffee and water, though. Not until the buyer arrived, anyway.

It was only the sight of a man in the doorway—one of the hotel's managers—that took Theo's attention away from the table for a split second. That was their signal for the start of the meeting, technically. It also meant, that by all visual accounts, the buyer had arrived as he had been told to. By an inconspicuous car, and with only one man by his side.

"Buyer has arrived."

Tommas shot Adriano a look, and without saying a single word out loud, his gaze said more than enough. *Here we go. No time for a fuckup, get it done.*

"Be open to negotiation on some aspects," Adriano said quickly, standing from the table with the rest of them—except Tommas; a boss stood for no one except another boss at his level, "give a little to get a lot, Tommas."

"We'll see."

He would, though. Adriano knew it. Tommas wanted this first contract to go off as well as the rest of them did. It meant more money for the Outfit, and in respect, for Tommas, too.

Next to his wife and son, there was fuck all Tommas liked more than money.

Soon, it was the buyer standing in the doorway. An initial meeting with the man months ago had given Adriano the chance to meet the man face to face. He was stockier, and tall. Mean-faced, but usually soft-spoken, which was a surprise.

Harold Torres' gaze drifted over the room before landing on them. The man behind him stayed two paces behind his boss, but it wasn't him that Adriano was interested in, but rather, the items hanging from the guy's grip.

Two black duffle bags.

Likely full of money.

What else would be in there? He'd been told after all what to bring, and how to bring it. And just the fact that the man had followed every single direction to a T told Adriano one thing only.

This meeting was going to go just fine.

The nod Tommas passed his way said the same. And also, a silent *well done* from his boss as well. Adriano finally felt like maybe he could breathe.

TEN

Eve and Theo

THEO

Theo walked in step with Damian just a few feet ahead of Adriano and Tommas. A good deal could do wonders for a mood, honestly. He looked forward to the changes this would bring to the Outfit over the coming years. While his work for the Outfit was at a higher level, keeping an eye on the boss and his business, Theo needed to get his hands a little dirtier. He missed really working—being in the thick of a job that kept him challenged as much as it entertained him.

He figured the guns were going to give him exactly what he was looking for on the side. And, of course, he'd keep up on his job of looking after Tommas' business.

As they neared the docks that would lead them down to their huts over the water, the conversation turned from the weapons they had just agreed to traffic to what would be left of their vacation.

"I vote on here again," Theo said.

"We're not coming here again," Damian muttered beside him.

"Are you still on the water thing?"

"*Yes.*"

Theo rolled his eyes. "The kids are fine—I told you that. We got everything locked and safe, just like you wanted. Pull that stick out of your ass, Damian, and have some fun for once."

"I have fun."

A scoff left Theo's lips. "*Rarely.*"

"Listen, it's decided," Damian said, "you and Eve are *never* planning another vacation again."

Theo scowled. "Why not? This place is great, asshole."

Tommas sighed loudly. "It is great. That's also not the problem."

"Then—"

"But it isn't very kid friendly," Adriano added.

Damian jerked a thumb over his shoulder. "That right there—see, I am not the only one who thinks so, Theo."

Theo's scowl only deepened at that, and he didn't bother to hide it, either. He made sure each and every one of them saw it for what it was because that was ridiculous.

"Listen, you fucking pricks, I am *not* going to Disneyland for my once-a-goddamn-year vacation, all right? I can't help the rest of you decided to go out and procreate right away."

Damian's hand came up fast to strike Theo in the back of the head playfully, but he dodged it just in time, and with his middle finger pointed up, too. "Smartass."

"I said what I said, dammit."

"Disneyland could be fun," Adriano said absently.

"Oh, my God," Theo groaned. "I am not going to fucking

Disneyland on the next vacation!"

Laughter from the other three lit up the docks, but Theo was busy mourning the loss of his youth, frankly. Somehow, he had managed to surround himself with *dads* as his friends. There would be no escaping it, he knew. This was going to be his life whether he had a kid or not. But he wasn't … having kids, that was.

Never.

He had all these people's kids to keep him entertained. That was enough for him.

Damian's arm snagged Theo around the neck, and dragged him in close. He managed to get his own swing in, landing a punch right to Damian's kidney.

"If we go to fucking Disneyland, you will go, too," Damian muttered through his laughter.

"I am *not.*"

"You will."

Yeah, probably.

He wasn't going to admit it out loud, though.

Finally, Damian let Theo go, and he took two wide steps sideways to get out of the fucker's reach. Pointing a finger between his eyes and then at his brother-in-law, Theo said, "I'm watching you."

"Good luck with that."

"Just admit you enjoyed the Maldives, Damian," Theo said, folding his arms over his chest. "Just say it—it's not hard. *Yes, Theo, I enjoyed the Maldives.* We're coming back here."

Damian pressed his lips into a thin line like he was trying to keep the words in, but eventually, he replied, "I never said I didn't like the place—"

"See!"

"And yes, once the kids are a little older, we will come back," his friend finished, cocking a brow. "But if you think I am flying with toddlers again on a regular flight like that first bright idea you and Eve had, you are fucking insane."

He didn't care about that.

He only cared about the other bit he heard.

Theo smirked. "A little older, huh? Like what, next year?"

"No, not next year. Maybe in a—"

Tommas cleared his throat, taking Theo and Damian's attention away from their argument for a moment. The two of them shot Tommas a look, but he only nodded in their direction. Or rather, past them, back toward their huts. Turning, Theo found exactly what the boss had been looking at.

Theo blinked.

And again.

Twinkle lights and tinsel lined the entire docks leading to their huts. Garland had been roped around the railings. Instead of just white sand, now it was a mixture of Christmas colors. Reds and greens. If Theo wasn't mistaken, that was mistletoe hanging over the front door to the first hut, too.

There wasn't a hell of a lot of Christmas decorations, sure, but it was just enough to make him chuckle.

Well done, Eve.

That was her only worry about this vacation. That somehow, Christmas would pass them by and no one would really celebrate it. Her favorite part of the holiday was decorating and making everything look like a fucking Christmas wonderland.

He supposed she'd done that again.

Just this time, in the Maldives.

That was his wife—always finding a way to get it done.

The four of them followed the twinkle lights and tinsel to the hut at the far end where the front door was wide open, and their wives moved between the hut, and the sitting area outside. Christmas music filtered out of Damian and Lily's place while the kids made sandcastles.

And where was Eve?

Down in the sand with the kids. Her bare legs were covered in sand, and she only laughed when Cory brought over a handful, and dumped it over her head.

Theo didn't want to interrupt his wife because clearly she was having the time of her life, so he hung back just far enough to watch her and hopefully stay out of her view. It only lasted as long as it took Joe to notice Theo was standing just around the corner of the hut watching them. The kid shouted his name, and Eve looked up with one of her blinding, sweet smiles.

"Hey," she said. "Wanna help me build a sandcastle?"

Theo laughed. "You look like you're doing great right there by yourself."

Did they really need two of them covered in sand? He didn't think so. That would be a whole battle and a half getting it all off her, but he bet he was going to enjoy every damn second of it, too.

"Did you like the decorations?" Eve asked, winking.

Theo nodded. "It's great, babe."

"I got a little tree in *every* hut, too."

Of course, she did.

He wasn't even surprised.

Now, everyone would have a place to put their gifts under before the night was out. Oh, he didn't think anyone had brought armfuls of gifts, but a couple for the kids, and probably one or two for their spouses. Once they got back to Chicago, they would have a huge Christmas party like always for everyone to exchange gifts and things … but here, there were only a few gifts to go around, as far as he knew.

"I still think you should come over here and help me build this sandcastle," she said teasingly.

Crossing the space between them, Theo bent down to place a kiss to the top of Eve's head. "No, but I still love you."

"You asked for it."

What?

Scooping a handful of sand up from the ground, Eve shoved it down the neckline of Theo's shirt before he could get away. Then, she grabbed tight to him, and brought him to the ground, laughing all the while. Right on top of her sandcastle, too.

Not that she looked like she minded.

On his back in the damp sand, staring up at the blue sky, Theo just shook his head.

Kids laughed all around him.

Eve smiled from up above.

Fuck it.

He'd go to Disneyland, too.

Why not?

ELEVEN

Abriella and Tommas

TOMMAS

"Did you like all those lights, huh?"

Tommaso nodded, holding tight to his father's hand. "Yeah, Papa."

Tommas grinned. "I bet. Did you help Ma decorate the tree, too?"

"I did. Put the star on top, too."

Chuckling, Tommas bent down to pick his son up. Balancing Tommaso on his hip, he headed into the hut with Abriella close behind. She wandered into the sitting area as he headed for the back where the beds were waiting for them. Or rather, Tommaso's bed was waiting for him. Tommas didn't need his son to tell him for him to know—the boy was dead tired.

All that excitement today had really done him in. That was the thing about kids. They spent their whole day in a constant state of movement and then when nighttime fell, they were out because of it.

Not that he was complaining.

Setting Tommaso on the bed, Tommas went about pulling all the curtains down to give the boy a sense of privacy. Plus, it helped to block out some of the light that was still shining in through the windows. It wasn't even dark yet, but that didn't matter.

It was eight.

Eight meant bedtime for Tommaso.

"Do you want Papa to read you a book before bed?" Tommas asked as he helped his son undress.

"No, I sleep."

Tommas smiled. "All right, buddy."

Soon, Tommaso was dressed, and under the covers. All that could be seen was his dark hair and bright blue eyes peeking out over the edge of the blanket as he stared up at his father.

"Papa?"

"Hmm, what?"

"Will Santa still find me?"

Kneeling down beside the bed, Tommas rested his arms along the edge and met his son's gaze. "Why wouldn't he, Tommaso?"

"I not home, Papa."

"Santa can find you *anywhere.* He's magic like that, you know?"

"How?"

"He just is."

"But why?"

Tommas laughed under his breath. *Fucking kids.* If he kept this conversation up with his son, Tommaso would find a reason to ask *how* or *why* for every single answer Tommas gave him. That's just how it worked with these little monsters.

"Santa is going to find you, I promise," Tommas said, leaning forward to press a kiss to his son's forehead before smoothing down his unruly hair with his palm. "But only if you go to bed like a good boy. Got it?"

"Okay, Papa."

"Night, little man. Love you."

"Night." Tommaso rolled over in his bed. "Wuv you, Papa."

He waited for an extra minute, until Tommaso's shoulders lifted and lowered rhythmically with even breaths. If the kid wasn't sleeping already, then he was damn close to it. Slipping out from behind the curtains without making a sound, Tommas was quick to find where his wife had set herself up.

In front of the small Christmas tree, Abriella sat cross-legged with a cup of green tea in her hands. She lifted the cup up to take a sip as Tommas came to sit beside his wife. Silently, he snaked an arm around her waist, and pulled her closer to his side. When even that wasn't enough for him, he pulled her into his lap altogether.

This was the best part of his day, usually. Quiet time with his wife when he could just enjoy her being close, and nothing more. Resting his lips on the back of her shoulder, he soaked in the silence and *her.* For a long while, the two of them said nothing, only watched the twinkle lights on the small tree blink and flicker with life.

Abriella broke the silence first. "He went to bed easily, then?"

"He's tired," Tommas murmured. "A lot like the rest of us, I think. Big day, baby."

He felt her nod, and then her hand came around to find his

clasped at her waist. Without saying a word, she unfurled his fingers, and snuck her palm in against his. Weaving their fingers tightly together, she held on tight to his hand. Tommas pressed another kiss to her shoulder just because he wanted to feel the softness of her skin on his lips.

"A big day is one way to put it," his wife said softly.

If there was one thing about Abriella that a lot of people didn't know, it was her strength and ability to *appear* fine even when it felt like her whole world was burning down around her. Not that their world was coming down around them, but it wasn't like his wife had been in the dark about this vacation, either. She knew there had been business going on behind the scenes even if she didn't ask too much about it. No doubt, she had been silently stewing in her mind over this whole thing.

Would it be okay?

Would this go bad?

And yet, she had never breathed a word to him either way about it. Maybe that was partly her raising, but he also liked to believe it was because of him, too. Not because he didn't allow his wife an opinion on his business or choices, but rather, he had proven time and time again that he would always walk back in through those doors to greet her at the end of every day.

So, she kept her worries quiet.

She let him go.

And she waited for him to come back.

Like all the times before.

"Ella," Tommas said, trailing kisses up the back of her neck.

"Hmm?"

He decided he didn't like talking to her like this. Not with her back to him, even if she was sitting in his lap. Snatching the cup of green tea from her hands, he set it aside, and turned her on his hip so that she was facing him. Her legs straddled his waist, he cupped her face, and brought her in for a slow kiss that had her grinning against his mouth.

"You know I'm always coming back," he told her.

She nodded. "I know … but it was Christmas, and we weren't in Chicago. I just got stuck in my head, I think."

"Ella."

She sighed. "I know, it's silly."

Not silly.

Understandable, really.

"I'm always going to be home for Christmas, too, Ella."

Abriella smiled. "I know, Tommy."

Good.

That's all he asked for, really.

TWELVE

Lily and Damian

DAMIAN

"Give it an hour, and they'll be sleeping hard," Damian said to Theo.

Theo chuckled. "They'll be fine, D. Don't worry about them."

Easier said than done. That was just a part of being a father, he figured. He was always going to worry about his kids whether he should or not. Even if was only leaving them for a couple of hours.

"And thanks," Damian added, "for coming over on Christmas Eve to keep an eye on them."

Theo shrugged. "We don't mind."

No, Damian supposed not. Theo and Eve were always quick to help someone with their kids whenever they needed it, and without complaint.

"How much longer are they going to be in the bathroom?" Theo asked.

Damian laughed. "Until Eve feels satisfied that Lily looks great."

His brother-in-law only shook his head, but said nothing. Where was the lie, though? Lily was happy just to get out of the hut with Damian for a couple of hours. She wouldn't have cared what she looked like or wore as long as she could put on one of those comfortable maxi dresses she liked. Eve, on the other hand, came over armed with a bunch of dress bags.

There was only the click of the bathroom door opening that drew Damian's attention back across the room. Lily came out of the bathroom wearing the same maxi dress she had gone in with, but her hair had been let down around her shoulders in soft waves. She wore little to no makeup, because frankly, Damian didn't think she needed it anyway but especially tonight.

"What were you even doing in there?" Theo asked. "She looks the same as she did before, Eve."

Eve shot her husband a look. "Talking—none of your business."

Theo only sighed.

Damian just chuckled. Fact was, Lily probably indulged Eve a bit, and then chose to wear what she wanted to wear. And he didn't even care as long as his wife was comfortable and happy.

"Ready whenever you are," Lily said, crossing the room to come to him. He held out a hand for her, and she took it without question, offering him a brilliant smile as she did so. He still loved her smile the best. That, and her legs. "And since you didn't tell me what we're doing, I hope what I am wearing is okay."

Damian grinned, and leaned in to catch his wife's lips with his own. Her mouth moving against him was a familiar dance, now, and he loved it the same way he always had. All too soon, he had to pull away because if he started this with her right now, they were never going to get out of here. "What you are wearing is perfect. Plus, I can always get it off if plans change."

"Yeah, that's enough of that," Theo grumbled. "Don't wanna hear that about my sister. Get out."

Waving a hand at Theo as if to shoo him off, Damian said, "In a minute."

Lily winked.

Damian kissed her again.

"Say goodbye to the boys first, right?"

"Sure, sweetheart."

Joe and Cory had set themselves up under the hammock with their trucks. For now, they were getting along. But how long that would last was anyone's guess, really. Lily kneeled down to say goodbye, and kiss both boys on the top of their heads. They were too interested in their game to realize their mother and father were leaving, but Damian considered that a blessing.

"Be good for Aunt Eve," he told his boys, "but give Uncle Theo hell, yeah?"

Cory grinned like he understood exactly what his father said. Joe, on the other hand, went back to quietly playing like nobody had spoken to him at all.

"I heard that," Theo muttered behind Damian.

He just waved a hand again.

Not wanting to waste one more minute, Damian grabbed tight to Lily's hand, and headed for the door without as much as a goodbye or even another thank you tossed over his shoulder. Lily's light laughter followed him out of the hut, and into the night air. They hadn't really gotten a single moment alone since coming on this vacation—he was not waiting one more second for five minutes with his wife.

"A little impatient, aren't you?" she asked.

Damian smirked. "You have no idea."

• • •

"Mmm, *fuck*."

Lily's high, breathless laughter colored up the boat. "I told you, didn't I?"

It was a hell of a lot harder for him to talk when his wife was seated on his dick, and the boat they were in was rocking like crazy from their frenzied fucking. Not that Damian was complaining because he sure as hell was not.

"You did. You told me."

Lily's sexy little smile colored up his vision. Well, her, and the black, inky skies with the stars in plain view splattered across the dark backdrop. Large on the horizon was a white moon that Damian thought, had never looked clearer or nicer.

"I was right, then?"

Damian grabbed tight to his wife's hips, and flexed his hips upward *hard*. He wanted to hear her sweet little gasps again when he filled her as full as he could get her. He loved the feeling of stretching her out with his cock. There was nothing quite like sex with his wife, really. Nothing compared.

This was heaven.

"You were right," he murmured, reveling in the way her pussy clenched around him as her mouth grazed over his jaw. "Sex definitely helped to take my mind off the water."

Or, he was going to let her believe that, anyway. He didn't really have a reason to worry about the water tonight, but when she climbed into his lap with a promise of fun and sin, he was not going to turn her away. Not when she was going to ride him until he couldn't fucking see straight or breathe right.

That was too good to pass up.

No man in his right mind would refuse.

Simple as that.

The tremors from Lily's last orgasm finally started to subside when her hips began to move again. Unlike last time, she didn't ride him hard and fast, though. No, she sat down on him until he was deep inside her, and then circled her hips into his lap just slow enough to drive him *crazy*. Her hands came up to cup his jaw, and then she was kissing him again. There was no mercy in her kiss—nothing easy or sweet about the way her tongue lashed inside his mouth to find his.

The kiss felt like war, really.

Never once did the movement of her hips slow. Even as her kiss burned him hotter, and he couldn't fucking hold onto her tight enough. Oh, he was going to come like this, and it was going to be insane.

God, he loved his wife.

• • •

"Okay, this better be good," Lily said. "When you said you had a surprise tonight, I didn't think you meant *this*."

Her voice was faint which told Damian she wasn't very happy at the moment. Or maybe it was just because he had put her on a boat, and blindfolded her.

"You don't even like the water, Damian."

He didn't.

At all.

But he did know how to steer a boat with a small engine, and he could fucking swim now. So could Lily. That took away a lot of the worry he had been feeling. Also, his kids weren't on the boat so that meant there were two other little people he didn't have to concern himself over at the moment. That all helped.

He chuckled. "I know, but this will be worth it, Lily."

"Can I take off the—"

"No."

His wife huffed, and he only grinned despite the fact she couldn't see it. A simple call to the trip advisor they had hired to arrange most of their vacation had given him all the information he needed to make this night perfect. He had the boat, he knew where to go and what time would be best to see the show, and had no doubt once he got his wife there, she would understand just fine why he had needed to blindfold her for the half-hour boat ride.

"Almost there," he promised.

Lily smiled a little, but kept quiet.

Damian hadn't been lying, though. It took another five minutes, but as soon as he steered the boat near the small island where a colony of plankton had gathered to grow near a beach. Keeping the boat back just enough that it wouldn't beach itself in the sand, he tossed out the cinderblock attached to a rope that would act as an anchor for them.

"Okay," Damian murmured, "I'm going to get you out of the boat. The water is going to be waist deep, so don't freak out."

"*What?*"

"Lily, I will be right there the whole time. It's only for a second, and then I will take your blindfold off. I promise."

"But—"

"Relax."

She sighed, but kept quiet as he helped her out of her dress to at least keep that dry for the moment. He made quick work of stripping down to the board shorts he'd slipped on earlier as well. First, he exited, then he helped to pull her down into the water, too. Once the two of them were in the water, and he had one hand tight on her waist, Damian reached up and pulled the blindfold off. It took Lily a minute, but once her gaze locked on his, he smiled.

"Keep looking at me, okay?"

"But why?"

"Just … for a second, sweetheart."

Lily smiled, and shook her head. "What are you even doing?"

"You'll see."

He led them closer to the beach, and all the while, Lily kept looking at him like he had told her to. He saw it first—the glowing plankton resting under the clear blue water. Given the dark skies, the plankton gave off a bright neon blue against the sand.

"Okay, go ahead and look, Lily."

He'd already seen the plankton, so he was much more interested in watching the way his wife's eyes lit up when she saw what he had brought her here for. The Maldives really were a special experience in that way—beautiful beaches, fantastic people to welcome them, and once-in-a-lifetime sights.

Kind of like this.

The glowing plankton seemed to stretch on along the quiet beach of the island for a good mile or two. Almost as far as their eyes could see, really.

Going in further until they were just ankle-deep, every step they took lit up the plankton even more. Lily laughed, bending down to trail her fingers through the water and sand, causing lines to glow like little trails from where she had touched.

"Oh, my God," she whispered. "That's amazing."

It was.

But she was better.

Standing straight again, Lily tucked herself into Damian's side. He kissed the top of her head, and when she tipped back to stare up at him, he kissed her lips, too.

"Merry Christmas, Lily."

"Merry Christmas, Damian."

THIRTEEN

Eve and Theo

EVE

"No, no, no, Cory," Theo said, his laughter echoing through the hut as he chased the naked toddler across the floor. Eve *could* have stepped in to help her husband, but watching him try to get Cory into the bathtub was way more fun. And far more amusing. "You swam in the water yesterday, didn't you? It's the same thing, kid!"

"Nos, Uncle Theo, nos!"

And with that, Cory threw himself to the floor, and immediately rolled under the bed just out of his uncle's reach. Eve listened as Theo tried to convince Cory to come out, and then when that didn't work, he thought using bribery might change the kid's mind.

"Uncle Theo will give you soda if you come out, Cory."

"Nos!"

"We won't tell Ma, either."

"Nos!"

"Get out here right now, kid."

"Nos!"

Eve let out a quiet laugh, but the second Theo's head popped up and his narrowed gaze landed on her, she pretended like she hadn't made a damn noise. He wouldn't appreciate her amusement at his troubles.

"You're still smiling, you know," he told her, "I can see it."

Was she?

Well, shit.

Eve tried to hide her smile by looking down at Joe as she ran a towel through his hair. A far easier child than his younger brother, Joe sat happily and quietly, all too willing to let his aunt get him ready for bed. He was easily pleased, and fine to follow the rules of his bedtime routine. Unlike his little brother.

"Ha!"

Theo's triumphant exclamation brought Eve's attention back to him just as he stood up from the floor with a wiggly, naked Cory in his arms. The kid kept his fight up all the way to the bathroom, never once letting his uncle think he truly had the upper hand on the child. And strangely enough, Eve knew that out of all the kids, Theo was most fond of Cory … even if he would never admit that out loud to her, or anyone else.

He never even considered playing favorites, and he never outwardly showed that he did have a favorite, but Eve knew her husband better than anyone. She could tell, even if he didn't say it out loud.

Maybe it was the kid's spirit.

Or his fight.

It could even be his attitude …

Whatever it was, she figured her husband found a lot of his own behavior and characteristics in the toddler and instead of getting annoyed with Cory, Theo just found himself amused by the boy's antics. Like what might come next?

It could be anything.

Eve already had Joe in bed, read his story, and watched him fall asleep before Theo finally got Cory bathed, dried, gave him his bedtime snack, and got him into bed. She was resting in the hammock with her e-reader when her husband finally came to stand beside her. Glancing up at him, she couldn't even hide her smile at the sight of his slightly tired eyes narrowing in on her.

"Is he finally asleep?"

Theo pressed his lips together. "Out like a light."

"I bet all that running away from you tired him out."

She couldn't stop herself from teasing him just a bit. What was fun about indulging his sulking? She would much rather make him smile a bit, anyway.

"You couldn't even help me, huh?"

She shrugged, and went back to her romance novel. "Don't act like you don't enjoy that kid, and his tricks, Theo. We both know you do."

It took him all of one second to reply, "Yeah, I really do."

"I know."

Without warning, Theo slipped into the hammock with her. It rocked dangerously, threatening to send both of them crashing to the floor as he resituated them both so that Eve was tucked into his side, and one of his feet dangled to the floor so that he could swing them back and forth. She barely kept in her shout of surprise, scared of falling, but somehow managed to keep quiet. If only because she didn't want to wake up the boys where they slept behind curtains that did *nothing* to keep out noise.

"Be careful," she whispered.

Theo chuckled deeply. "We're fine."

And they were.

His arm snaked around her, and pulled her closer as she opened up her e-reader again, and went back to the story of a virginal heroine who had just ran into her crush—who also happened to be her brother's best friend. God, she loved that trope.

But it was a lot harder to focus on her book when Theo was this close. Not that she minded, really. His fingers drifted over the bare skin of her arm as his lips grazed her hairline.

"We're definitely coming back here, right?" she asked.

"First chance we can, babe."

Eve smiled. "Good."

Maybe next time, they would come alone. Or maybe everyone would come again. Who knew? Eve didn't really care as long as Theo was there with her. He made *everything* so much better.

"You know, I have all those gifts for the kids to wrap when we get back to the hut," Eve said, grinning up at her husband.

Theo rolled his eyes. "I suppose I could help you with that."

"Yay!"

"Like you didn't plan that this whole time."

Eve shrugged, not even ashamed of her trickery. "You wrap presents far nicer than I do, anyway."

"That is true."

"Your ego is huge."

"No lie there, either," he murmured.

"Good thing I love you."

"Yes, that is the good thing."

"So, it's a deal, then," she said.

"What is?"

"You'll wrap *all* the presents for me when we get back?"

"Hey, that is not—"

"Too late," she crowed. "You agreed."

Theo's fingers went from drifting over her skin to tickling her for all he was worth. Her muffled giggles quieted when he turned her over so that she was resting on his chest, and pressed his lips against hers.

Giving her a wink, he murmured against her lips, "Fine, I'll wrap all your presents for you."

"I knew you would."

"But I expect something in return."

His voice dipped sinfully.

Eve wet her lips, replying, "I guess we'll see what I can do for you."

Anything, really.

She'd do anything for him.

FOURTEEN

Abriella and Tommas

ABRIELLA

"Took you two long enough," Abriella grumbled as she opened the front door to her hut to let Theo and Eve inside. "Everyone is ready."

Theo and Eve, with both their arms loaded with wrapped gifts, at least had the decency to look sheepish about being late. They'd all agreed to meet at Tommas and Abriella's hut for Christmas morning to open gifts, and make breakfast. Everyone else but these two had managed to show up on time, and surprise, surprise, they were the only ones without kids, too.

At the same time, Abriella had no interest in learning exactly why they were late … she was pretty sure she could guess that all on her own. Likely the same reason she didn't like to get out of bed in the mornings because someone beside her was all too happy to keep her under the sheets with him.

"Well, we're here now," Theo said, grinning at Abriella as he passed her by, "so let's get these gifts to the kids, and somebody put me in the kitchen because I am fucking *starved*."

Abriella side-eyed the man. "Are you going to help cook, too?"

Theo at least had the decency to act shocked that she would even ask that question. "Of course."

"Mmhmm, Tommas is already in there with Damian getting everything ready. Feel free to join them."

She helped Eve to unload some of the gifts for the kids, making sure that each child had their own pile of gifts in an effort to keep them from tearing into somebody else's gifts. Although, Abriella didn't think the kids would care, really. Next to Joe, the rest of the little ones were still at an age where the paper and boxes the toys came in were far more interesting than the toys themselves. The adults would likely be the ones to open up most of the gifts.

Abriella sat down with Tommaso as he struggled to get the paper off the corner of one of his gifts. Sure, there weren't a lot of presents. Four to each child—one from everyone, basically, but it was enough. They were going to have to travel with all this shit home, too. Even if they were taking another private jet.

Plus, there was a big, red Santa bag with a gift for each child, too. But once they got home, there would be a whole bunch of presents and fun waiting.

Because yeah, Tommas was not even messing around for the trip back. Abriella was grateful for that, though. Less stress, really.

"You want Ma to help?" she asked Tommaso.

Her big, blue-eyed boy nodded. "Thanks, Ma."

Pulling Tommaso into her lap, she grabbed the present from his hands, and tore off the side that had been giving him the most trouble. Once she gave him that little bit of help, he was easily able to tear the rest of the paper off to reveal the gift from Damian and Lily. A model Hummer, by the looks of it. One that matched the Hummer he had seen parked in their driveway during their last party, and went crazy over because it was so big, and his favorite color—yellow.

Like a Hummer wasn't ostentatious enough, the person had to paint it yellow, too. Just like the model Hummer in the box. Or rather, the pieces of it.

According to the box, the Hummer was in fifteen-hundred pieces that would need to be put together. Approximate time to put together, over thirty hours.

Wow.

Abriella saw Lily grinning at her from the side, and shook her head. "Thanks, really."

"Deny he's going to love that."

"Oh, he'll love it. Tommas … not so much when he's the one putting it together piece by piece."

Lily shrugged. "But what are dads for, though, right?"

Good point.

And Tommaso did love it. He was more than content with sitting on his mother's lap and looking over that box for as long as he could. Suddenly, he didn't seem to have any interest with the other three gifts waiting for him on the floor, not even when his mother tried to entice him with the promise of a train being in one because that's what she and his father had gotten him.

He loved trains, too.

Abriella figured it didn't matter, anyway. He'd get around to his other gifts when he was good and ready, even if it took a while. She enjoyed watching the other kids tear into their gifts, or in the case of Alessa and Adriano's daughters, have their mother open up each gift for them before demanding she open each one for them to play with.

By the time the kids had gotten into each of their gifts—including Tommaso—she could smell bacon, eggs, and all the other goodness that the guys had prepped for breakfast. Tommas came up behind her with a smile. Tipping her head back, Abriella grinned.

"All ready?"

"Whenever you are, baby," he said.

Oh, she was definitely ready to eat. And given the fact she could hear Tommaso's little belly rumbling, even if he was fine to be distracted with his model Hummer, he was ready for some food, too.

"Look, Papa," Tommaso said, holding his toy up proudly. "Sees?"

Tommas took the Hummer from his son, and eyed the box. "That looks like something Papa is going to have a hell of a time with, actually."

Across the floor, Damian chuckled. "Remember to wear gloves, Tommy. I hear the glue is hell to get off."

Her husband shot his cousin a quirked brow, but Damian only shrugged his broad shoulders. Setting the box back to the floor, Tommas bent down and said to Tommaso, "Go find a seat in the kitchen, and I'll get you some food, buddy."

"Okays."

Abriella let her son scramble out of her lap, but before she too could get off the floor, her husband pulled out an item he had been keeping hidden behind his back.

A single piece of mistletoe he must have pulled down from their decorations. He held it over her head, and winked.

"Is it really Christmas," he started to say, "if someone doesn't get a kiss under the mistletoe, Ella?"

She grinned. "It isn't, no."

"Didn't think so."

Dipping his head down, he dropped a quick kiss to her lips.

Merry Christmas, that kiss said.

"Maldives and Mistletoe," she whispered against his mouth. "Kind of appropriate, isn't it?"

"Kind of perfect, actually."

FIFTEEN

Lily and Damian

LILY

Lily rested on the square-shaped hammock suspended from the back veranda of her hut where it hung over the water. Given Christmas was going to be their last day in the Maldives, she had every intention of enjoying what was left of their time here. On one side of her, Alessa was baking in the sun and ignoring her sister's warnings about sunscreen. On the other side, Eve had rolled over to her stomach to tease Theo where he was swimming just a few feet away.

She wasn't sure where Damian was, but she could hear his laughter in the background so that told her everything was just fine. She didn't need to move, and that was her entire goal today.

"Then at least put on a hat," Abriella said from where she sat shaded on the back veranda. "You'll regret this in ten years when you have a sunspot or two, Lissa."

"All your complaining is what I'm going to regret, Ella."

Lily and Eve muffled their laughter to keep Abriella's glare from turning on them.

Eve pushed up on her elbows. "Let her enjoy herself, Ella."

Abriella huffed.

"You know what we should do," Lily said, peering up at the sky that was so clear, all she could see was bright blue for miles, "is head into town tonight, find a club, drink and dance all night."

"Been a while since we did that," Eve agreed.

"Adulting *sucks*," Abriella muttered.

"What about the kids?" Alessa asked.

"They have dads," Lily deadpanned.

"So, it's decided, then?" Abriella grinned slyly. "We go out and have fun, and the rest of them stay here and watch the kids?"

"It's agreed," the three from the hammock echoed.

"I'm not drinking," Alessa added after a minute. "But I'll go and dance."

Lily glanced over at her friend. "Why wouldn't you want to have a drink with us? I know you brought your pump for the baby—you could get her milk for the night and morning ready, and then she'd be fine."

Having a drink was part of the *fun*.

Alessa opened her mouth to reply, but it was only the sound of arms cutting through water that stopped her. Theo had finally decided to pay back his wife for teasing him minutes ago, it seemed. A wave of cold water came up behind the hammock, and landed on all of them, not just Eve.

"Theo!" Eve shouted. "You asshole!"

"That's what you get for thinking you could tease me and leave it be, Eve. Doesn't work that way with me," Theo taunted.

Lily turned in just enough time to watch her brother swimming away from them, but not before he tossed a cocky smirk over his shoulder. His chuckles echoed over the water. Lily glared at her brother for all she was worth. She tried really hard *not* to hope a shark would come up and bite him on the ass, but it was difficult.

They were having such a good time sunbathing on the hammock, and now they were all soaked. All that work Lily put into managing her hair that just did not seem to like this heat was now ruined.

"He gets Cory again," Lily said, narrowing her gaze on her brother. "That's who he gets to watch tonight."

Laughter passed over the girls, because hell yeah, they all knew how troublesome Cory could be when he wanted to make someone's life difficult.

Eve and Alessa were already climbing off the hammock just as Abriella came out of the back of the hut with towels ready for them. Lily soon followed, still grumpy that now she looked like a damn mess. By the time she had gotten dried off, and slipped her shawl over her shoulders, the others had headed in the house to get drinks for the kids playing outside.

She was going to help, but then she heard the laughter of her boys, and Damian. It was like an invisible rope had suddenly been tied around her middle, and was tugging her in their direction. It was funny how that worked; her husband was trying to give her a little bit of time to relax as this was going to be their last day here, and somehow, Lily just found her way right back to her boys and husband, anyway.

She wouldn't have it any other way.

Lily came around the side of the hut to find her husband chasing after a laughing Joe while still keeping hold of a squirming Cory under his arm like a football. Nobody was getting in any trouble, it seemed. They were all laughing like there was no tomorrow. Including little Cory who didn't seem to have any problem with being tucked under his father's arm while Damian chased after Joe.

"Get back here, Joe!"

"No tickles, Da, no!"

Lily hung back just out of sight, so she could watch the three of them play. There was something about all her boys being together and having fun that made her smile. She hoped, as the years went by and these little ones of hers got older, that they still took time out to do exactly *this*. Have fun with each other. She wanted them to never take life too seriously. To find the good in even the bad. To *live*.

After all, hadn't the rest of them suffered and sacrificed enough so that these kids—this next generation of Outfit kids—wouldn't ever have to?

She thought so.

Sometimes, in moments like this when she had the chance to watch from afar, Joe and Cory really reminded her of Theo and Dino. Not that she remembered her brothers at that age, because she didn't. But there was something in the way they looked, and how they acted with one another that just hit the feeling of it right on the head. Like a memory she could feel, but couldn't see in her mind.

It made her miss her oldest brother a great deal. She wished he could be here to see her kids grow up the way he watched her grow up. She never talked about it with Damian, or even her brother because well, Theo never asked. Maybe she just wasn't ready to have that conversation, either.

Wounds like those healed, sure, but they were still sore to the touch.

Lily glanced upward—at the sky, to find the heavens out of reach. She supposed … as long as Dino was happy, then the rest didn't matter. He was just another one of them who had suffered, and so, she knew he was another one who needed to have his peace.

Simple as that.

It was only Damian catching Joe finally with a triumphant *whoop* that brought her out of her musings. Both of her sons' laughter filled up the yard, high and breathless. It skipped over the sand to her spot, filling her heart with a happiness like nothing before as Damian got both boys to the sand, and tickled one with each hand.

They had rules, though.

They were teaching *boundaries*.

The second the boys said *no* or *stop*, their father did just that. Because how would they ever learn to respect someone else's body when as a child—even with something as simple as tickling—they had been taught their body wouldn't be respected?

Damian scooped up both boys, and found the closest spot he could sit down with them. That just happened to be a log they'd all been using as a makeshift bench. Joe sat on one side of his father trying to catch his breath and grinning all the while, and Cory sat on the other side, smiling up at his dad like his whole world revolved around Damian.

Lily bet it did revolve around Damian, too.

Damian picked Cory up to set him in his lap, and Joe moved a little closer to his father as well. It struck Lily silent for a moment as she looked at her boys—one lighter-haired, and the other darker.

Day and night, really.

One quiet, the other, loud and proud.

She slipped the phone out of the pocket of her shawl as she came around the corner, and her three boys looked her way with wide smiles. She already had the phone up and ready to take a picture, her thumb hovering over the button to capture the perfect image in front of her.

"Don't move," she told Damian, "and keep them smiling for me."

Throughout their entire vacation, she had not been able to get one *really* good picture of the three of them together. Cory was always moving too fast, or Joe was too interested in something else.

Kids were fun that way, she supposed.

But this here …

Perfect.

Lily took the picture, and smiled as she peered over the captured image of her boys.

"Best Christmas present ever."

SIXTEEN

Alessa and Adriano

ALESSA

"Are you sure you don't want me to stay just in case they don't stay in bed?" Alessa asked.

Adriano chuckled as he pulled the darker curtains closed around their two kids. The girls had already been put to bed, and had been sleeping for a good half an hour, but that didn't matter. As much as she wanted to go out and have fun with the girls, she also wanted to stay right here with Adriano and her girls.

Mom guilt was a bitch.

Funny how that worked.

"Lissa," Adriano said, crossing the room to where she was sitting on the couch, "it's fine, babe."

"Yeah, but—"

"Go have fun with the girls, and enjoy the last night here. Okay?"

Alessa sighed, and smiled up at her husband. "Love you, huh?"

Adriano grinned, but the sight wasn't anything new. He'd been smiling like that ever since he got his business out of the way on their vacation. Once he knew his deal had gone through and without a hitch, the man eased into this vacation like he had never had any worries to begin with.

She didn't really have to wonder why, though. This was a big thing for Adriano, and he'd once again proved that just because he was younger than a lot of the men he worked with, he could still get his job done, and do it well. She wished he didn't feel the need to prove himself as much as he did, but she was happy to support him no matter what he chose to do.

She was his wife.

What else could she do?

Besides, happiness was a good look on him, really.

"Come here," she whispered.

Adriano leaned down, and rested his hands on either side of her thighs. Those fingers of his pressed into the bare flesh of her thighs where her skirt had ridden up just enough. Maybe it was all the hormones, or the changes they caused, but his touch was enough to send flames licking along all of her nerves.

Alessa reached up to cup his jaw, and drag him close enough that she could actually *kiss* him. She loved the way Adriano's lips worked against hers—soft at first, teasing and tasting. And then rougher the moment she parted her lips to let him deepen the kiss. His tongue darted in to find hers, and the world shifted.

Things became a little more beautiful.

She had no control with this man.

None whatsoever.

A single kiss from him had her yanking him closer until she was able to get him down on the couch, too. Climbing onto his lap, she was quick to yank her dress higher before working at his pants. If she wasn't so interested in getting one thing from her husband in that moment, she might have found it amusing how he didn't even care that their simple kiss had turned into something far hotter for no particular reason.

Well, no reason that he knew.

For now …

"Jesus Christ."

Adriano grunted when Alessa finally got his cock free. In her hands, he was smooth and hard. His cock pulsed with every stroke of her fingers down his shaft. She knew just when to squeeze to really get him making all those husky, sexy sounds she loved, but right then, she didn't have the patience for any of that. She wanted *one thing*, and that was to get this man inside her.

He was all too happy to move her panties aside, his knuckles grazing her already-wet sex as she lifted above him. In the next breath, she was lowering on him, getting what she wanted the most, and nothing had ever felt better. There was something about the way he felt filling her up, and stretching her out that drove Alessa crazy.

It got better every fucking time.

"Oh, my God," she breathed.

His hands found her ass, and his lips trailed over her jaw. A hard squeeze to her backside had her grinding in his lap while hot kisses drifted over her skin.

Warmth and bliss spread through her body like a wild fire. There was no escaping it, but she was all too happy with letting it ravage her anyway. Adriano gave her a second—one to breathe and get accustomed to the sensation of him settling a little deeper inside her pussy, and then he was moving again.

Flipping them both over on the couch so he could pound into her the way she liked best, Alessa couldn't seem to take in enough air. Pleasure licked over her skin—pulling her muscles taut, and promising relief was soon to follow. It was harder than she thought it would be to keep those sounds of hers locked up tight—God knew they didn't want to wake the sleeping girls in their makeshift room.

Adriano saved the day by stuffing two of his fingers in Alessa's mouth. She sucked on his digits, her teeth biting down on his knuckles to keep those noises of hers at bay.

And then she was coming.

Hard.

Fast.

Blinding.

It came on quicker than she realized, like the edge was suddenly there, and she was flying over it without anything below to catch her. Alessa didn't mind falling, not when it meant Adriano was coming with her.

And he did.

His fingers slipped from her mouth as he buried his face into her neck, his thrusts came a little harder, and then his muffled grunt echoed against her skin. She felt him spill deep inside her clenching sex as he held her tight at her waist, and kept her pinned down to the couch all the while.

"Fuck," he mumbled.

Alessa laughed breathlessly. "Well, that worked out just fine, didn't it?"

Leaning up a bit, Adriano lifted a brow. "I'd say so."

He dropped a kiss to her grinning lips.

"I bet I'm late now—they're probably waiting for me to come out."

"Yeah, we always wait on them, though."

True.

Sometimes.

"Oh," she murmured, her grin deepening. "I have one more surprise for you. One last Christmas gift."

Adriano quirked a brow. "Do you now?"

"Mmhmm."

"Where did you keep it hidden? Because I helped you pack everything, and I didn't see anything."

"Well, what if I bought something while we were here?"

"But you didn't because you didn't leave the huts, Lissa."

Damn man.

He was too smart for his own good.

Alessa was just a little bit more sly than him, though. "I didn't get anything—Abriella went and got it for me yesterday when she went to town with Tommas."

"What are you—"

She didn't give him the chance to finish his question before she pulled an item out of the pocket of her dress that had somehow managed to stay put even through their fast, frenzied fucking. Lucky, really. That's why she loved dresses with pockets.

They held all kinds of secrets.

Flashing the item in front of her husband's eyes, Alessa watched as Adriano's whole face *lit up*. A smile split his lips, and reached his eyes. A happy laugh fell from his lips.

"Really?" he asked, staring at the pregnancy test she held.

Alessa nodded. "Really."

He dropped a kiss to her mouth, then her nose, forehead, cheeks … everywhere he could reach, really. Alessa's laughter lit up the hut, she couldn't even try to hold it back. Not that she wanted to, honestly.

"This was the best Christmas yet," Adriano murmured against her lips when he found his way back there.

Alessa smiled into his kiss.

The very best.

A NOTE!

Well, loves … I intended to write this Chicago War Christmas Novella for you last year, but life always has a way of getting in the way, doesn't it? So this year, I made sure to get Maldives & Mistletoe done in lots of time so that you could read it in time for the holidays, and celebrate with the original crew from Chicago one last time.

I mean … maybe?

Who knows if this will be the last novel from this group. I am hoping to maybe write a book for Chloe from the original books, and Cory from the second generation. So this may not be the last you see of all of them just yet.

Thank you for coming along on this ride with me, loves.

Happy reading.

BK.

ABOUT THE AUTHOR

Bethany-Kris is a Canadian author, lover of much, and mother to four young sons, one cat, and three dogs. A small town in Eastern Canada where she was born and raised is where she has always called home. With her boys under her feet, a snuggling cat, barking dogs, and a spouse calling over his shoulder, she is nearly always writing something ... when she can find the time.

Find Bethany-Kris at her:

WEBSITE: www.bethanykris.com
BLOG: www.bethanykris.blogspot.com
FACEBOOK: www.facebook.com/bethanykriswrites
TWITTER: www.twitter.com/bethanykris
INSTAGRAM: www.instagram.com/bethany.kris
PINTEREST: www.pinterest.com/bethanykris

Sign up to Bethany-Kris's New Release Newsletter here: http://eepurl.com/bf9lzD.

OTHER BOOKS

Andino + Haven

Duty
Vow

John + Siena

Loyalty
Disgrace

Cross + Catherine

Always
Revere
Unruly
The Companion
Naz & Roz

Guzzi Duet

Unraveled, Book One
Entangled, Book Two

DeLuca Duet

Waste of Worth: Part One
Worth of Waste: Part Two

Standalone Titles

Effortless
Inflict
Cozen
Captivated
Dishonored

Donati Bloodlines

Thin Lies
Thin Lines
Thin Lives
Behind the Bloodlines
The Complete Trilogy

Filthy Marcellos

Antony
Lucian
Giovanni
Dante
Legacy
A Very Marcello Christmas
The Complete Collection

Seasons of Betrayal

Where the Sun Hides
Where the Snow Falls
Where the Wind Whispers
Seasons: The Complete Seasons of Betrayal Series

Gun Moll Trilogy

Gun Moll
Gangster Moll
Madame Moll

The Chicago War

Deathless & Divided
Reckless & Ruined
Scarless & Sacred
Breathless & Bloodstained
The Complete Series
Maldives & Mistletoe

The Russian Guns

The Arrangement
The Life
The Score
Demyan & Ana
Shattered
The Jersey Vignettes

Find more on Bethany-Kris's website at www.bethanykris.com.

www.ingramcontent.com/pod-product-compliance
Lightning Source LLC
Chambersburg PA
CBHW072034170626
46811CB00008B/3081

9781988197760